Megan McDonald is the author of the
popular series starring Stink's sister, Judy Moody.
She says, "Once, while I was visiting a class, the kids
chanted, 'Stink! Stink! Stink!' as I entered the room.
In that moment, I knew that Stink had to have a
book of his own." Stink now has his very own series.
Megan McDonald lives in California.

You can find out more about Megan McDonald
and her books at **www.meganmcdonald.net**

Peter H. Reynolds is the illustrator of all
the Judy Moody and Stink books. He says, "Stink
reminds me of myself growing up: dealing with a
sister prone to teasing and bossing around – and
having to get creative in order to stand tall beside
her." Peter H. Reynolds lives in Massachusetts.

You can find out more about Peter H. Reynolds
and his art at **www.fablevision.com**

Stin

Megan McDonald   illustrated by

K and the Midnight Zombie Walk

Peter H. Reynolds

WALKER
BOOKS

for all the booksellers
and readers at Copperfield's
M. M.

To Elizabeth Morton
and her mum and dad
P. H. R.

First published 2012 by Walker Books Ltd
87 Vauxhall Walk, London SE11 5HJ

This edition published 2013

2 4 6 8 10 9 7 5 3 1

Text © 2012 Megan McDonald
Illustrations © 2012 Peter H. Reynolds

Stink ™. Stink is a registered trademark of
Candlewick Press, Inc, Somerville MA

The right of Megan McDonald and Peter H. Reynolds to be identified
as author and illustrator respectively of this work has been asserted by them
in accordance with the Copyright, Designs and Patents Act 1988

This book has been typeset in Stone Informal

Printed and bound in Germany

British Library Cataloguing in Publication Data:
a catalogue record for this book is available from the British Library

ISBN 978-1-4063-4704-3

www.stinkmoody.com
www.walker.co.uk

CONTENTS

Guts!

Brains!

Eyeballs!

"Take that. You're dead," said Fred Zombie.

"I'm not dead. I'm *un*dead," said Voodoo Zombie.

Stink and Webster were playing Attack of the Knitting Needle Zombies when Fred Zombie's eye fell off and rolled across the floor.

"Holy eyeball!" yelled Stink.

"Hey, where did you get these way-cool zombies, anyway?" said Webster.

"When I was, like, five, my grandma Lou made me monsters out of yarn. So I turned them into zombies. See? This one still has a needle in his head."

"Stick a needle in his eye," said Webster. "Sick."

"One more week," said Stink.

"One more week," said Webster.

"One more week till what?" asked Judy Moody, Stink's big sister. Sometimes she was such a Nosy Parker.

"DUH! The Midnight Zombie Walk!"

Stink and Webster said at the same time. Stink pointed to the website.

**ZOMBIES INVADE
BLUE FROG BOOKSHOP
THIS SATURDAY! 9 P.M.
Book Release Party for
Nightmare on Zombie Street, Book Five
Only $12.99! Order your copy today.
Going faster than canned brains!
Midnight Zombie Walk to follow book
sales – at the stroke of 10!**

Webster pointed to the countdown clock. "See? Only seven more days!"

"Book Five. *Creature with the Cootie Brain,*" said Stink.

12

"Zombies. Cootie brains. What's so great about those books, anyway?" Judy asked.

"Only *everything*!" said Stink.

"They're funny," said Webster.

"And gross," said Stink.

"And creepy," said Webster.

"Vomitocious!" said Stink and Webster.

"And they have comics at the end of every chapter," said Stink.

"And they count for reading points towards the one million minutes," said Webster.

"Our school is trying to reach one

million minutes of reading," said Stink.

"Hel-lo! I know! I go to the same school," said Judy. She waved a Nancy Drew book in front of them.

"See, there are four zombies, named Hoodoo, Voodoo, Gilgamesh and Fred. And they speak in Zombie," said Stink.

"Yeah, in Zombie everything starts with a *Z*," said Webster.

"Like, your name would be Zudy Zoody, my zorky zister," said Stink.

"Very funny, Zink!" said Judy.

"In Book One, super-galactic alien zombies from outer space descend on Braintree, Massachusetts, and take over Nightmare Street," said Stink.

"And in Book Two, the zombies can't get enough brains. So they take over fifth-grade break! Fifth-grade brains are juicy."

"Then there's *Dr Decay and the Zombies of Doom*. In that one, Hoodoo gets bitten by this evil zombie, Dr Decay, and his brains are all hanging out and—"

"Gross," said Judy. "I didn't ask for a book report!"

"You'd like it," said Stink. "There's even a Band-Aid–crazy zombie, like you."

"You guys have zombies on the brain," said Judy.

Webster picked up Hoodoo and Voodoo. "We're going to brain you!" Hoodoo and Voodoo said to Fred.

"We eat brains!" said Stink.

Fred attacked Voodoo. "Mmm, mmm, good."

"Brains for lunch," said Webster. "Munch, munch munch-a-roni."

"And breakfast. And dinner. Body parts. Yum. We love body parts!"

"Somebody ate *your* brain, Stink, if you think you're going to a Midnight Zombie Walk," Judy said.

"Why?"

"Hel-lo! Mid-night! That means staying up as late as Santa on Christmas Eve."

"So? I can eat a whole bunch of

Zombie Zitz and get hyper and stay awake past midnight."

"Actually, the walk starts at ten o'clock," said Webster.

"Ten o'clock is *so* not midnight," Judy said. "Besides, it says here you have to buy the new zombie book to get in. Books cost money. Twelve dollars and ninety-nine cents each."

"Twelve ninety-nine plus twelve ninety-nine. That's like ... ninety-nine dollars," said Stink.

"Twenty-five dollars and ninety-eight cents, to be exact," said Judy. "You spent all your money on that video game, *Zombietron 4.3.* Where are you guys going to get twenty-five dollars and ninety-eight cents?"

Stink crossed his arms. "No sweat. I have a plan."

"Don't you mean a *brain*storm?" Judy asked.

"Good one," said Stink.

"Your plans stink," said Judy.

Stink cracked up. "My plan *does* stink."

"It does?" Webster asked.

"Of corpse. The smelliest," said Stink. Stink and Webster rolled on the floor laughing.

Judy made the cuckoo sign. "You guys know you're a little weird-o, right?"

"A little weirdo? Well … your *brain* is little," said Stink. "At least we don't have pea brains." He held up two fingers to show the absolute pea size of Judy's brain. "Teeny. Tiny. Weeny brain."

"The better *not* to get eaten by a zombie," said Judy.

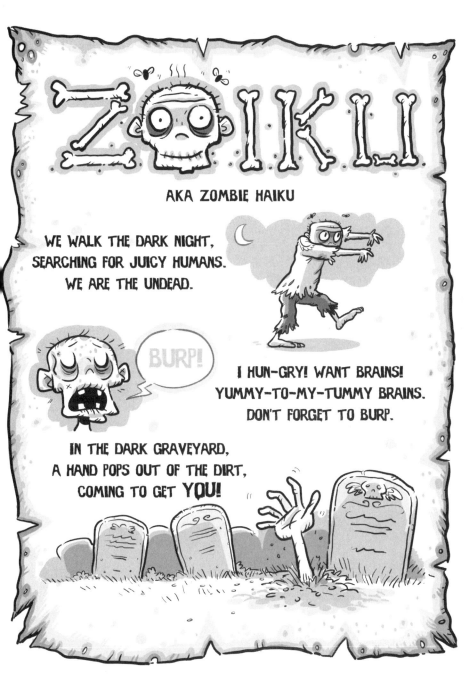

On Monday after school, Webster asked Stink, "So what's your plan?"

"Plan? What plan?"

"The super-smelly plan that's going to make us ninety-nine gazillion dollars. So we can both buy the book? So we can go to the Midnight Zombie Walk?"

"Don't have one."

"But you said…"

"I just said that to mess with my sister."

"We need a *not-fake* plan," said Webster.

"Let's think," said Stink. "Two brains are better than one." He slurped a brain-shaped sucker. Webster munched Zombie Zitz and Candy Scabs.

Ding! "I know," said Stink. "Let's have a blowout garage sale and sell all our old stuff. Like action figures we don't play with any more."

"Yeah! We can sell dinosaurs, cowboys, Mr Spud Head, Debbie Dump Truck, my old Handy Andy and Buzz Lightspeed. Too preschool."

"Deal," said Stink.

* * *

Webster ran home to raid his closet. He came back with a big box. In the box was one old marble, a toy lizard without a tail and a plastic egg.

"That's it?" asked Stink. "This is *so* not going to make us rich."

"Giving away stuff is harder than I thought," said Webster.

"Tell me about it," said Stink. He pointed to the small pile on his bed. One Poky Little Puppy, a broken light saber and a Red Robot pencil sharpener.

"Actually, I think I want to keep the pencil sharpener," said Stink.

"Forget it," said Webster. "Judy's right. This plan stinks."

"The stinkiest." Stink sharpened pencils with his Red Robot. Pencil shavings littered the floor. They looked like moth wings. He picked them up and sniffed. They smelled good, like trees.

"Wait a second," said Stink. "Maybe I *do* have a stinky plan after all."

"What is it?"

"We sell smells," said Stink.

"Shells?"

"No, smells! We get a paper cup, right? We put smelly stuff in the cup. Then we charge fifty cents for people to smell it."

"What people?"

Stink shrugged. "Any people."

"But who's going to give us money just to smell stuff?"

"You'll see. People love to smell stuff."

"People don't love to smell *skunks*."

"But we can sell *good* smells, like … berries and dirt and stuff. No skunks. And *no* corpse flowers."

"Who will pay us to smell dirt?"

"Riley Rottenberger. She likes anything rotten."

"Riley Rottenberger would pay to smell putrid rotten burgers," said Webster.

★　★　★

Stink set up a table in the garden and lined up his smell cups. Candy cane, pinecone, cinnamon, fruit gum, dirt and soap.

"Soap?" asked Webster.

"What? It smells good. Like lemons."

Also pencil shavings and eraser crumbs. Stink made a sign. 50¢ A SMELL. He set a fancy dish on the table. He put one dollar in the dish.

"The secret to selling stuff is to put some of your own money out. People see it, and they'll pay money to smell stuff too. Plus the fancy dish makes it look like a real shop. Trust me."

"Fifty cents a sniff!" yelled Webster.

"Two for a dollar!" Stink called to anybody who came down the street. Mrs Ling, the neighbour. Jack Frost, the postman. But they all said, "No, thanks."

"Fifty cents a smell," Stink called to a kid on a bike.

"But I can smell stuff at home for free. I'm smelling free stuff right now."

"Nah-uh," said Stink.

"Ya-huh. Air."

"This isn't working," said Webster. "Let's give up."

"We can't just give up," said Stink. "New ideas take time. It's a known fact that it takes seventy-two hours for a human being to like a new idea."

"It does?"

"Sure. Everybody knows that. Just like everybody knows that smell is the best out of all five senses."

"It is?"

Sheesh. Sometimes his best friend sure was behind the Magic 8 Ball.

"What's all this?" Judy asked, coming outside. She picked up a cup. She took a sniff. She made a face. She took another whiff.

"One dollar," said Stink. "Hand it over. You took two whole smells."

"We're selling smells," said Webster.

"Then you owe me *two* dollars for stealing my bowling pin eraser set." Judy held up the cup full of eraser crumbs.

"Great," said Webster. "Now we're

in the minus instead of the plus."

"Does Mum know you're using her good dish?" Judy asked.

"Nothing is going to happen to Mum's dish. I swear!"

"It's *your* life," said Judy, heading back inside.

Stink and Webster waited. Not one person came down the street. Not one car drove by. Not one whiff. Not one sniff.

"Has it been seventy-two hours yet?" Webster asked.

"Wait," said Stink. "Let's turn this into a Smellatorium!" He picked up a

cup and wrote *Zombie Toe Jam.* Eraser crumbs were now *Zombie Zits.*

"Do zombies have B.O.?" Webster asked.

"The worst! Duh!" said Stink. "They're dead!"

Webster wrote *Zombie B.O.* on a cup. Soon each cup was a zombie smell.

"Step up to the Smellatorium, if you dare," called Stink.

"Zombie zits, farts and B.O.!" yelled Webster.

Kids lined up at the table. In no time, the boys had a dish full of quarters.

"Two dollars," said Stink. "Zombie Walk, here we come!"

"No way. That's only enough to pay Judy back for the erasers," said Webster. Just then, Stink saw Missy, the neighbourhood dog walker. She had four leads and four dogs.

"Hi, Missy!" Stink waved. "Hi, Max, Molly, Bella and Missy!"

"I thought Missy was the person," said Webster.

"She is. But the other Missy is that Chihuahua."

All four dogs tugged on their leads. They barked. They pulled Missy the

Person across the street to Stink and Webster's Table of Smells.

The dogs barked and leapt and jumped. "Down, boy," said Missy. "Bella! Max!" She tugged on their leads.

"Want to smell?" asked Stink. "It's only fifty cents per sniff."

"And it's for a good cause," said Webster.

"What's the cause?" asked Missy.

"Zombies," said Stink.

Just then, Bella and Max leapt up on to the table. They went crazy sniffing. Their leads got all tangled.

"The dogs are smelling for free!" said Webster.

"Bella! Down, girl. Bad dog, Max!" said Missy the Person.

She pulled on their leads and *CRASH*! The fancy dish fell off the table and

smashed to pieces on the pavement.

Stink's mouth hung open. Webster's eyes bugged out of his head.

"I'm so sorry, Stink," said Missy the Person.

"It's…that's…my mum's," said Stink.

"I'll pay for it, of course," said Missy. She dug in her backpack. "How much do I owe you?"

"Twenty-five dollars and ninety-eight cents," said Stink and Webster at the same time.

"Plus tax." Stink grinned.

Missy held out her hand. "Will you take four dollars, a cough drop and a purple paper clip?"

At school on Tuesday, Stink tapped Sophie of the Elves on the shoulder. "Hey, So—"

Sophie turned around. She had smears and smudges of green all over her face. And green streaks in her hair.

"Why is your face green?" Stink asked.

"Face paint," said Sophie. "I couldn't get it all off."

"Why were you wearing green face paint?"

"Zombie," Sophie whispered, and turned back around.

Stink almost jumped out of his seat. "Zombie! You're into zombies too?"

"Of *corpse*," said Sophie. "Shh! Mrs D.'s looking. Talk later."

✳ ✳ ✳

At lunch, Stink and Webster sat across from Sophie. Stink took out his baloney sandwich. With ketchup.

"Welcome to the vomiteria," said Sophie. Stink and Webster cracked up.

"Wouldn't it be weird if all of a

sudden the cafeteria served brains?"

Suddenly Stink's pink baloney and red ketchup did not look so good. "Freaky-zeaky," said Stink. He munched on an apple instead.

Sophie opened her lunch box. She took out one cheese sandwich, carrot sticks, a box of raisins and ... zombie!

"Meet Zombalina!" said Sophie.

Stink and Webster stared at a ten-centimetre tall fairy with a ghost-white face, black-rimmed eyes and freak-out hair. Her skirt was made of blood-streaked Band-Aids.

"What happened to Blossomina,

Rider of Unicorns and Friend to All Elves, who rids the world of evil sprites?"

"Sprites, schmites," said Sophie. "Blossomina is Zombalina now!"

"Since when?"

"Since I read Nightmare on Zombie Street Books One and Two this weekend."

"Do you know about the Midnight Zombie Walk at the Blue Frog Bookshop this Saturday?" asked Webster.

"Why do you think I have green paint on my face? I've been trying to figure out a zombie costume to wear."

Riley Rottenberger butted in. "I'm going as a prom queen zombie."

"Do you even know what a zombie is?" Stink asked.

"It's like a princess," said Riley, "only she wears black instead of pink."

"A *dead* princess," said Sophie.

"Do we have enough money for the books yet?" Webster asked Stink.

"Let's see." Stink ticked it off on his fingers. "We have four dollars from Missy, ten dollars from your birthday money, my five-dollar-off voucher…"

"That's not enough for two books," said Sophie.

"Plus the two dollars we got in quarters if we don't pay Judy back, plus the one dollar we put in the dish. If you count in my allowance, that's more than twenty-five dollars and ninety-eight cents."

"Yesss! We are so there!" said Webster.

Just then, the head teacher came into the lunchroom. "Boys and girls," said Ms Tuxedo. "I have some exciting news. We have just reached nine hundred and seventy-six thousand four hundred and thirty-three minutes of reading!"

The cafeteria exploded with clapping and cheering.

"Only twenty-three thousand five hundred and sixty-seven more minutes to go. Now, I know many of you have been reading the Zombie series, and there's a new one coming out on Saturday, so I would like to declare this Friday Read to a Zombie Day."

The lunchroom went wild.

"Zool!" said Stink.

"Second- and third-graders will read aloud to K-1 kids in their classrooms. That'll go a long way towards reaching our goal of one million minutes by Saturday. Don't forget to join us at the Blue Frog Bookshop on that day to celebrate all our great reading!"

Riley Rottenberger raised her hand. "What about B.O.B.?"

B.O.B. was the Big Orange Box outside the front office. Nobody knew what was inside. It was a surprise.

"Tell you what," said the head

teacher. "If Virginia Dare School reaches one million minutes, I promise we will have the Big Orange Box moved to the bookshop on Saturday, and finally, at last, once and for all, open B.O.B.!"

"Bob, Bob, Bob, Bob, Bob," the kids chanted.

When the room had quietened down, Stink asked his friends, "What do you think is in there, anyway?"

"Maybe B.O.B. really stands for *Big Overstuffed Bear,*" said Sophie.

"A Big Overstuffed *zombie* teddy Bear!" said Webster.

"Or *Box of Bears:* three hundred and ninety-seven teddy bears, one for each kid at Dare School," Riley butted in.

"Or maybe B.O.B. stands for *Big Oversized Brain,* and there's zombie brains in there or something," said Webster.

"Or something," said Stink.

"Sweets," said Webster. "Ten hundred tons of sweets."

"Bookmarks," said Sophie. "Teachers love bookmarks. And pencils."

"B.O.B. is for *Big Old Bookmarks?*" Stink asked. "That stinks."

"I guess we'll just have to wait till

Saturday night to find out," said Sophie. "Until then, I can borrow Book Three from the library and Book Four from you guys, and Book Five I can get on Saturday 'cos it's almost my birthday."

"Zweet!" said Stink.

"That will be worth like a zillion reading points," said Webster.

"My house. After school," Stink said. "We can help each other with our costumes. My sister has boxes of body parts and stuff."

"Is she a zombie?" asked Sophie.

"Only *most* of the time," said Stink.

"Zee you there," said Webster.

8 WAYS TO TELL IF YOUR SISTER IS A ZOMBIE

GROAN!

1. SHE PALE AS GHOST.

2. SHE SEE JELLY, SAY "GOT BRAINS?"

3. SHE GRUNT. SHE GROAN.

4. DEAD SKUNK BREATH. P. U.

5. SHE NOT BLINK. WINS STAREDOWN CONTEST.

6. SHE WALK LIKE ROBOT.

7. SHE EAT KETCHUP, SAY "MMM. BLOOD!"

8. SHE STAY UP ALL NIGHT.

Sophie and Webster came over. Stink was sitting on the floor with Toady in his lap. He fed his toad two freeze-dried mealworms.

"I brought face paint," said Sophie. "So we can practise zombie makeup."

"I brought bloodshot eyeballs," said Webster. "They're really for bike spokes but we can glue them on to stuff."

"And I have tofu, erasers and Silly Putty," Stink told them. "Stuff that looks like brains. And glow-in-the-dark gummy worms for maggots crawling all over us."

Sophie shivered.

Webster decided to dress like a zombie football player. Sophie was going to be a zombie Girl Scout. Stink could not decide on a costume.

"It has to be scary. And creepy." He opened his lunch box. He took a bite of leftover baloney and ketchup sandwich. Toady croaked.

Stink's elbow knocked over the puppet that was sitting on his desk chair. The puppet had great big glarey eyes, creepy red lips and scary eyebrows. And it was wearing a tuxedo.

Sophie picked up the puppet. "You could dress up like this doll. He's creepy."

"Charlie's not a doll. He's a dummy. A ventriloquist dummy."

"A whosie whatsit dummy?" asked Webster.

"Ven-tril-o-quist. You know, like a guy with a puppet who can throw his voice. See, I make Charlie talk without moving my lips."

"Let's see!" said Webster.

Stink sat Charlie on his knee.

"I may be a dummy," said Charlie, "but I'm not dumb." His head snapped back and forth. His mouth clacked open and shut. "And I'm not afraid of zombies."

Sophie cracked up.

"I saw your lips move," Webster said, pointing at Stink.

"Hey, let's zombify Charlie!" said Stink. Stink dropped his baloney sandwich. Plop! Out fell the baloney. Toady hopped out of his lap.

Stink took out scissors and cut

Charlie's tux to shreds. Sophie painted Charlie's face green, with black circles under his eyes and drips of red blood. Webster stuck a big gob of chewed-up ABC gum on Charlie's head for brains.

Stink held up Charlie. "Me. Zombie."

"He's a little scary," said Sophie. "Toady's scared, too. Look at him go!" Toady hopped across the rug, heading straight for the baloney.

"Spooky!" said Webster, shaking off a chill. "Charlie's like the dummy in that freaky old movie. The one where he hides in the kid's closet?"

"Yipes. I think I have auto-ma-ton-o-phobia," said Stink.

"What's that?" asked Sophie and Webster.

"Fear of dummies. No lie."

All of a sudden, Stink heard a creepy sound. The heater hissed. A clock ticked. The pipes moaned. The light buzzed. *Pop!* Stink saw a flash, and the bulb in his desk lamp burned out. The room went dark.

"Aagh!" Stink tossed Charlie up in the air and jumped up to flick on the overhead light.

"Look! Charlie! Zombie!" said

Webster in a shaky voice, huddling in the corner. Sophie gasped.

Charlie was sitting on Stink's race-car bed, head backwards, one black and bloody eye open.

Webster leaned in closer. "Did he just say something?"

"Did who just say something?" Stink asked.

"Charlie."

"You mean did I just say something to make Charlie say something?"

"Huh? Yes. I mean, no. I don't know."

"What did you hear him say?"

"I heard him say *baloney*."

"I didn't make him say *baloney*."

"Who said *baloney*?" Sophie asked.

"What did you make him say?" Webster asked Stink.

"I didn't make him say anything," said Stink.

"Ha, ha. Very funny, Stink," said Webster.

"Seriously," said Stink. "I thought one of *you* guys said *baloney*."

"I didn't say *baloney*," said Sophie.

"I didn't say *baloney*," said Webster.

"Judy," said Stink. He looked out into the hall. No sign of his sister.

"Well, if *I* didn't say *baloney* and *you* didn't say *baloney,* and *Sophie* didn't say *baloney,* and *Judy* didn't … then…" Stink felt zombie goose bumps up and down his back.

"AaaHHH!" he screamed, and pointed to something pink hopping across the floor.

"Did you see what I saw?" Stink asked.

"The baloney! It … moved!" said Sophie.

"It's undead!" said Webster.

"Curse of the zombie baloney!" Stink yelled, flailing his arms.

The three friends got up, zoomed out of the room and slammed the door behind them.

"Phew. That was a close one," said Webster. "Let's never go back in there."

"But we left Toady in there … with Evil-Eye Charlie!" said Sophie.

"I have to save him," said Stink. "I'm going in." He cracked the door open. He looked around. No sign of Toady.

"The zombie ate him!" said Webster. "Toad soup!"

"Toad *brains*," said Sophie.

Stink stared at the undead baloney. It was no longer moving. It was still as a stone. But it had a big lump under it.

Stink crawled over to the baloney. He reached out a hand. Quick as a wink, he lifted up the baloney. "Toady!"

"Toady was attacked by the zombie baloney!" Webster shouted.

"That does it," said Stink. He put Toady back into his tank. "This room is now a zombie-free zone." He grabbed one-eyed Charlie and tore out of his room.

He dashed across the hall into Judy's room. He yanked open her closet and hid Charlie at the way-bottom of the clothes basket, under heaps of dirty laundry.

Phew! Safe from talking dummies and walking baloney with a curse on it.

For now.

ZOMBIFY YOURSELF

WANT TO LOOK UNDEAD? HERE'S HOW:

- SMEAR ON WHITE OR GREEN FACE PAINT.

- WEAR PURPLE OR BLACK LIPSTICK.

- USE RED LIPSTICK TO DRAW BLOOD DRIPPING FROM YOUR MOUTH.

- DRAW BLACK CIRCLES AROUND YOUR EYES.

- TAKE SCISSORS TO AN OLD T-SHIRT. SHRED 'ER UP!

- A LITTLE KETCHUP GOES A LONG WAY— FOR BLOOD SPATTERS.

- ALWAYS CARRY A BODY PART WITH YOU— TRY A DOLL HEAD, LEG OR ARM.

On Wednesday and Thursday, Virginia Dare School read books. Funny books. Mystery books. Adventure books.

Kids read at lunch. They read at break. They read at after-school club. Even between football games and piano lessons.

Stink read to Toady. Stink read to Astro. Stink read for one hundred and eighty-seven minutes in just two days!

At last it was Friday: Read to a Zombie Day! Stink ran downstairs. He popped a waffle into the toaster. "Where's my lunch?" he asked Mum, looking for his lunch box. "I'll have anything but baloney, please."

"I, uh, thought you and Judy could get hot lunch today," said Mum. "I've left some money on the table."

"Aw, Mum. You know I hate hot lunch. The lunch lady always makes me take mountains of spinach and piles of wrinkly old carrots."

"It won't hurt you to eat school lunch just this once. Who knows?

Maybe today will be your lucky day and they'll serve something really interesting."

"You mean like mini cupcakes with no sneaky carrots in them? And no raisins?"

"Remember how we talked about eating more fruit, Stink?"

"Bus. Bye!" said Stink. He grabbed the money, gave Mum a kiss and ran out of the door.

*　*　*

Stink read *Dr Decay and the Zombies of Doom* all the way to the bus stop. He read it on the bus. He read it in the hall on the way to Room 2D.

"Hey, Zink!" somebody called.

"Talk. Bad. Read. Good!" said Stink.

Morning announcements. "Attention zecond- and zird-graders," said the head teacher. "Are you ready to read to a zombie? Only six thousand four hundred and ninety-three minutes to go! Please make your way down to the K-1 classrooms. Let's get reading!"

"I've read for two hundred and

forty-seven minutes so far this week," Sophie told Stink.

"Way to go!" said Stink. "Now there's only six thousand four hundred and ninety-nine minus two hundred and forty-seven minutes to go!"

When Class 2D got to the kinder-garten classroom, twenty-two little green-faced zombies were sitting cross-legged on carpet squares. There were zombie princesses and ballerinas, pirates and astronauts.

Stink sat down next to a boy named Zack in a train outfit. "I'm Thomas the Tank Zombie," said the boy.

"I like your costume," said Stink. "I've never seen a zombie train before."

Zack nodded. Stink started to read. He read *The Very Hungry Zombie Caterpillar.* It was just like *The Very Hungry Caterpillar,* only he threw in the word *zombie* a lot. And at the end, the caterpillar ate a brain instead of a green leaf.

Riley Rottenberger went to get more books from the library. When she came back, she whispered to Heather Strong. Heather whispered to Webster. Webster whispered to Sophie. And Sophie whispered to Stink.

"A zombie ate the lunch lady?" Stink blurted out loud.

The room fell dead silent.

"Shh!" said Sophie. "You'll scare the little kids."

"A fourth-grader told Riley when she was in the library," said Webster. "Fourth-graders don't lie."

Class 2D was buzzing with the rumour:

"Zombies have taken over the cafeteria."

"Zombie Island!"

"All the food is gross and putrid."

"Great," said Stink. "Of all the days

my mum makes me get hot lunch."

"Mine too," said Webster.

"Mine three," said Sophie. "She made a big deal about it."

"Same here," said Stink. "Now we're going to have to eat *brains*."

Mrs D. held up two fingers. "Boys and girls, I'm proud of all the great reading here today. Thanks to your help, we've just added over four thousand more minutes to our reading challenge!"

"YAY!"

"Lunchtime, second-graders," said Mrs D.

Nobody moved. Nobody stood to line up.

At last, one brave soul stood up: Riley Rottenberger. "You guys! Do you *really* think there's a *zombie* in the *cafeteria*? Right here at Virginia Dare School?"

"No," Stink said out loud. But inside there was a tiny little *yes*.

Stink and the rest of the second-graders walked down the hall. Stink could not help imagining a giant alien zombie taking a bite out of Mrs Swanson, the lunch lady.

When Stink got to the cafeteria,

everything *seemed* to be normal. Except for the banner that read VOMI-TERIA in pukey green letters.

Then he stepped inside.

Gadzooks! The windows were swamp-green. The tables were puke-green. And gross green stuff was hanging from the ceiling. "The cafeteria got slimed!" said Stink.

"And it smells like a swamp," said Webster.

The Vomiteria buzzed with excitement. Everybody was talking at once.

Stink grabbed a tray. He started to go through the lunch line. He read the board that said:

TODAY'S MENU:

- SCRAMBLED BRAINS WITH A SIDE OF GUTS
- ZOMBIE FRIED RICE
- SPLEEN STEW
- SLOPPY TOES ON A BUN
- EYEBALL SOUP
- SPAGHETTI MEDULLA WITH DRIPPING BLOOD SAUCE

"Eeuw. Everything looks like insides," said Webster.

"That s-s-soup is s-s-staring at me," said Sophie.

"I think I feel the pukes coming on," said Stink.

"Welcome to the vomiteria," said a voice. A *zombie* voice.

"Aah!" Stink, Sophie and Webster jumped. They stared wide-eyed at the Zombie Lunch Lady behind the counter.

Her face looked three-years dead. She was wearing an apron that read GOT BRAINS? It was covered in bloody

handprints. Plus it had human ears, a nose and a hand stuck to it. Not to mention that she had a meat cleaver coming out of her head!

"Scrambled brains with a side of guts, anyone?" asked the Zombie Lunch Lady. She held up a slotted spoon. It was drip-drip-dripping with ... blood?

"Vomitocious!" Stink pulled his tray back. "Is there anything that doesn't smell like a corpse flower?"

"Excuse me, um, Mrs Zombie?" Sophie asked. "Do you have any milk?"

"Zorry. No milk. We do have eyeball juice. Freshly squeezed."

That voice. "Mu-umm?" Stink asked.

"Mrs Moody?" said Webster and Sophie.

Mum grinned. "Hi, kids. What do you zink?" She twirled in a circle, showing off her zombie costume.

"*You're* the zombie that ate the lunch lady?" Stink asked.

"Truth? I didn't eat anybody. But I did tell some fourth-graders that a zombie ate the real lunch lady and took over the cafeteria. All foods today are on the zombie food pyramid."

"You're like the coolest mum ever," said Sophie.

"So this is why you made me get hot lunch today?" asked Stink.

Mum couldn't help smiling. "It was my turn to serve hot lunch, so a couple of other parents and I thought it might be fun to dress up for Read to a Zombie Day. Mums and dads will do just about anything to encourage reading. How'd it go this morning, by the way?"

"We read over four thousand minutes!" said Stink.

"Great job!" said Mum. "You kids

have really been working hard on your reading."

"Thanks," said Sophie.

"Are those real insides?" Webster asked.

"Taste and see," said Mum. "What'll it be? Spaghetti? I mean, brains? Or Sloppy Toes?" She whispered to Sophie, "Sloppy Joes?"

All three kids held out their trays.

"Scrambled brains," said Webster.

"Sloppy toes," said Sophie.

"Eyeball soup, please," said Stink.

ZOMBIE AFTER-SCHOOL SNACKS
ZOMBIES NEED BRAIN FOOD TOO!

THE SEVERED HAND

POUR JELLY INTO A RUBBER GLOVE.
(SPRAY IT WITH COOKING OIL FIRST!)
TIE THE END CLOSED AND FREEZE.
CUT AWAY THE GLOVE.
SERVE FLOATING IN LEMONADE OR PUNCH.

HOLY EYEBALLS!

CUT SOME HARD-BOILED EGGS IN HALF.
SCOOP OUT THE YOLKS AND REPLACE THEM
WITH CREAM CHEESE AND ONE OLIVE.
DON'T FORGET TO MAKE THE EYES BLOODSHOT
(DRIBBLE SQUIGGLY LINES OF RED FOOD
COLOURING ON THE CREAM CHEESE)!

BERRY BLOODY SMOOTHIE

MAKE A SMOOTHIE BY BLENDING
CRANBERRY JUICE WITH ANY RED
FRUIT SUCH AS STRAWBERRIES,
RASPBERRIES OR WATERMELON.

MORE ROTTEN IDEAS:
PEELED GRAPES MAKE GREAT EYEBALLS.
GUMMY WORMS = MAGGOTS
MINI HOT DOGS MAKE GOOD "FINGER" FOOD. *HARDEE-HAR-HAR.*
DRIED CHERRIES OR CRANBERRIES DOUBLE AS SCABS!

On Friday night, Midnight Zombie Walk Eve, Stink and Webster had a sleepover. A zombie sleepover!

They put on their zombie pyjamas (striped pjs with ketchup stains). They played Zombie Attack with Fred and Voodoo. They watched *Night of the Living Bedspread* and ate *finger* foods dipped in blood (mini hot dogs dipped in ketchup). They told zombie jokes.

"Why did the zombie cross the road?" asked Webster.

"To eat the people on the other side."

"How did the zombie get an *A* on his test?" Stink asked.

"It was a no-brainer!"

Stink and Webster crawled into sleeping bags and reread Nightmare on Zombie Street books by torchlight.

Judy poked her head into the room. "Hey. Tofu-for-Brains," she said to Stink. "Mum and Dad said lights-out. Time for bed."

"But we're not tired," said Stink. "Tell us a story."

"A zombie story," said Webster.

"A scary zombie story," said Stink.

"But not too scary," said Webster.

"'Nightmare on Croaker Street,'" said Stink.

"*One* story," Judy agreed. "If you promise to leave me alone and get some Zs."

"Zs for zombies," said Stink.

Judy made her voice all spooky. "One night, two boys were having a sleepover. A zombie sleepover."

"Did they live on Croaker Street?" Stink asked.

"Can their names be Webman and Stinkray?" Webster asked.

"Shh!" said Judy. "One night, Webman and Stinkray were having a sleepover."

"Nice," said Stink.

"You guys can't keep interrupting me, or the story won't work."

Webster shut his mouth.

Stink zipped his lips.

Judy went on. "All of a sudden, there came a *scritch-scratch-scritch* on the window."

"Was it a zombie?" asked Webster.

"Yes. It was a zombie. She had looong black hair and a pale, pale face and red, red lips and looong green fingernails. Her voice was like dead bones rattling. 'Do you know what I do with my red, red lips and my looong green fingernails?' she said."

Judy flicked the torch on and off. "'NO!' said Webman and Stinkray, and they slammed the window shut."

Stink and Webster sat up in their sleeping bags. They inched closer to Judy.

"The next night," Judy continued, "the zombie came back and she said, 'Do you know what I do with my red, red lips and my looong green fingernails?'

"Again Webman and Stinkray said 'NO!' and they slammed the window shut.

"On the third night, the zombie asked the same thing: 'Do you know what I do with my red, red lips and my looong green fingernails?' But before

Webman and Stinkray could answer, she said, 'I'll SHOW you what I do with my red, red lips and my looong green fingernails.' Webman and Stinkray closed their eyes and held their breath. Finally, the zombie held her finger to her lips and went: 'Blubblubblubblub blubblubblub.'"

"That was funny," said Stink.

"And scary," said Webster.

Judy turned off the torch. "Night, you guys. Sweet dreams." She clomped downstairs.

Wind whistled at the window. The moon made spooky shadows on the wall.

"Did you hear a scratching at the window?" asked Webster.

"Maybe it's just a tree branch," said Stink.

"Are you scared?" asked Webster. He hugged Hoodoo and Voodoo.

"A little," said Stink. He pulled Gilgamesh and Fred in closer.

"I can't sleep," said Webster.

"I have an idea. Let's scare Judy like she scared us!"

"How?" asked Webster.

"It's a no-brainer," said Stink. "Charlie Zombie! He's in her closet, remember? So we sneak into her room and get Charlie, and then we hide somewhere in her room. When she comes up to bed, we make Charlie Zombie talk and freak her out."

"I like it," said Webster.

Stink and Webster tiptoed across the hall and into Judy's room. Stink fished Charlie Zombie out from the bottom of Judy's washing basket in her closet. Charlie looked as creepy as ever.

Webster hid behind Judy's beanbag chair. Stink and Charlie hid under the bottom bunk.

"Night, Mum," they heard Judy say out in the hall. She came into her room and climbed into her bottom bunk. She pulled up the covers and turned to face the wall.

They waited for five long minutes. Slowly, Stink raised the dummy out from under the bed. Slowly, slowly, Charlie rose up in the blue moonlight. His face glowed green in the dark like

a ghost. He stared at Judy with one eye open and waited.

Judy stirred. She rolled over.

Clack-clack-clack! went the dummy's mouth. Judy opened one eye.

"Hun-gry," Charlie Zombie croaked. "Want burger. Ju-dy bur-ger!"

"Aagh!" Judy screamed, and she pulled the covers over her head. "AAGH!" she screamed again.

"Scared you!" yelled Stink. Stink and Webster popped out from their hiding places, laughing their pj pants off.

"You guys!" said Judy, poking her head out from under the covers. "I almost had a zombie heart attack!"

"Heart. Yum," said Charlie.

Webster cracked up.

"We got you so good," said Stink.

"You'd be scared too if some creep-azoid zombie dummy woke you up in the middle of the night," said Judy. "Get that thing out of here." Judy pulled her covers back up.

Stink and Webster headed back to Stink's room.

"Scritch-scratch!" she called after them. "I wouldn't sleep near the window if I were you."

Stink set Charlie Zombie back on

his desk chair. He and Webster slid back into their sleeping bags and closed their eyes.

"Webster? Are you thinking what I'm thinking?" Stink asked.

"He's staring at us," said Webster. "With one evil eye."

"I know. His other eye won't stay open. He's giving me the creeps."

"Goose bumps," said Webster, rubbing his arms.

"Goose eggs," said Stink.

"Zombie zits," said Webster.

"We're going to have zombie nightmares!" said Stink.

He got up and switched on his night-light.

"Put a pillow over him or something," said Webster.

"I'll get him out of here." Stink took Charlie all the way downstairs, where he stuck him way in the back of the hall closet, behind all the coats.

At last, Stink and Webster slipped off to sleep. Not a creature was stirring, not even a zombie.

✳   ✳   ✳

The next morning, Stink woke up. Webster woke up.

Stink yawned. Webster yawned.

Stink screamed, "AAAGH!"

Webster screamed, "Zombie!"

Charlie the One-Eyed Zombie was leaning against the pillows on Stink's bed, staring at them and grinning his evil grin. Stink and Webster huddled together. "He's back!" said Webster. "When did you—?"

"I didn't," said Stink. "Did you?"

"Not me."

"But ... how did—? I hid him in the way-back of the downstairs closet!"

"AAGH!" Stink and Webster ran screaming out of the room.

Stink and Webster ran screaming down the stairs.

Dad poked his head out of the kitchen. "What's all the racket?"

"Nothing," said Stink. "We just" – he sniffed the air – "smelled pancakes."

"Pancakes. Good," said Webster.

"Me want," said Stink.

Dad went back into the kitchen.

"Did you know that zombies have a hyper-good sense of smell?" Stink said to Webster.

"Then we'd better hurry up, before Charlie Zombie beats us to them."

Countdown! One, two, three, four, five more hours until the Midnight Zombie Walk!

Stink read seventeen minutes of the Z encyclopedia. He read thirteen minutes of zombie books. He read eleven minutes of comic books. Forty-one minutes of reading!

He played with Astro for twelve minutes. He practised karate for thirty-three minutes. He bugged Judy for twenty-six minutes while she worked on her Doctor Zombie costume.

At last it was time!

Stink put on his zombie ventriloquist costume. He painted his face green. He drew red blood coming out of his mouth and ears with lipstick. He put on his top hat. "C'mon, Charlie. Time to go."

When the Moodys got to the Blue Frog Bookshop, zombie princesses and cowboys, pirates and superheroes crowded the pavement. Stink saw his teacher, Mrs D., and tons of kids from Virginia Dare School.

"Is that the queue?" Judy asked. "It goes all the way to Screamin' Mimi's!"

"Zombies, zombies everywhere!" said Stink. He waved to Mrs D.

"It's great that so many teachers from your school are here," said Mum.

A teenager bared his fangs at Stink. "I vant to vite your veins! Mwa-ha-ha-ha."

"Vampire-free zone," said Stink, drawing an invisible circle around himself. "Zombies only."

Stink found Sophie and Webster. "Zow-ee!" he said, pointing to the football boot sticking out of Webster's head. "Insane in the membrane!"

"Undead in the head!" said Webster. They cracked up.

Sophie of the Elves was now Zophia of the Girl Scouts. Even Zombalina was dressed in a mini green uniform. "Check out my badges," Sophie said, pointing to her sash. "Zombie First Aid. Zombie Cookie Sales. And Zombie Friendship. You know, because zombies always stick together and travel in packs."

"Why did you put tape over the campfire badge?" asked Webster.

"Duh! Because zombies hate fire!"

"Zool," said Stink. "What time do they zopen the doors?"

"Nine o'clock zharp," said Dad, checking his watch.

"What time is it now?"

"Eight fifty," said Dad. "Ten more minutes."

"Zen more minutes," said Stink. "That's like an hour in kid years." He pressed his nose to the window of the bookshop. "Just think, in ten minutes, I'll be holding Nightmare on Zombie

Street, Book Number Five, in my very own hands. In ten minutes, I'll be reading the actual brand-spanking new, just-released, way-official *Creature with the Cootie Brain*."

"Your brain has cooties," said Judy.

"What time is it now?" Stink asked Dad.

"Eight fifty-three," said Dad.

"And twenty-two zeconds," said Mum.

Stink waved his hands at the door of the bookshop. "Open Zombie!" he commanded. The keys in the front door went *jingle, jingle*. The door went *click*!

"Wow, I must have super magic zombie powers," said Stink.

"Welcome to the Midnight Zombie Walk!" said the bookshop lady.

"Cootie brains, here I come," said Stink. He, along with crowds of other kids, pushed through the doors. "Is this zombie rush hour or something?"

"Or something," said Judy. She reached up to steady her Bridezilla wig.

While they waited, Stink and Judy spotted B.O.B. at the back of the bookshop. B.O.B. was wrapped in a big green bow.

When it was Stink's turn, he sat Charlie Zombie on the counter and made him talk: "Zombie. Want. Book!" Charlie moaned at the book-shop clerk.

"He'd like Book Number Five, please," Judy said, translating.

The bookshop lady handed a brand-spanking-new book to Stink. Stink handed over his money.

"Whoa! *Creature with the Cootie Brain!*" Stink sang. He could not help doing a little "I got it" dance with his feet. Then he held the book to his nose and took a whiff.

"Stink. You're smelling a book," said Judy.

"So? New-book smell is the best."

"Don't forget your *free* zombie cootie catcher," said the bookshop lady.

"Zombies use them to catch human cooties before they eat your brains."

"Zank you," said Stink.

Nightmare on Zombie Street, Book Five. *Creature with the Cootie Brain.* Page One. *A strange darkness fell over Zombie Street...*

For ten minutes, a strange quiet fell over the bookshop. Zombies short and tall, cheerleader to cowboy, had their noses in books. Big zombies read to little zombies. Dad and mum zombies read quietly to kid zombies.

Stink could not stop reading Book Number Five. *Fred went pale. Hoodoo* and *Voodoo clutched each other. "This is your last warning," said Gilgamesh. "Beware the creature with the cootie brain!"*

Stink finished chapter 1.

Ding ding ding! "Attention, everybody! May I have your attention!" said the bookshop lady. "I have an important announcement to make. I've just been told that one of our local schools, Virginia Dare Elementary, has reached one million minutes of reading!"

The crowd went wild. Zombies clapped and whooped and hollered.

Stink's teacher, Mrs Dempster, stood

up. "To any Virginia Dare students here tonight, your teachers are proud of you. You've all worked really hard. Your parents are proud of you, too, but no one is prouder tonight than Ms Tuxedo, the head teacher of Virginia Dare Elementary."

A buzz went through the crowd.

"Where is she?"

"Where's the head teacher?"

"Ms Tuxedo could not be here with us tonight," Mrs Dempster continued.

"Awww!" everybody yelled.

Mrs D. walked over to B.O.B. "So she has asked me to do the honours on her behalf, and open the Big Orange Box."

"Bob!" screamed the crowd. "Bob! Bob! Bob! Bob! Bob!"

Mrs D. held up a pair of scissors. A hush fell over the crowd.

Snip! Mrs D. cut the ribbon.

Mrs D. grinned. *Voilà!*

Mrs D. opened one flap, then the other. The crowd held its breath.

Out of the box popped a haystack of half-black, half-white hair. Zombie hair! And the hair was perched on top of ... person! That person began to sing:

"Cruella De Zombie, Cruella De Zombie.
If she doesn't freak you out, nothing will."

Cruella De Zombie wore a black-and-white spotted coat and blood-red boots. With a sweep of her arm, she tossed a black feather boa over her shoulder. A giant eyeball necklace gleamed in the spotlight. Next to her was a real-live dog – a Dalmatian, with a fake bloody arm in its mouth.

"Head Teacher Tuxedo!" everybody yelled. The zombie head teacher held the eyeball up to her eye. "I vant to zee some reading!" The crowd went bonkers.

"Boys and girls," shouted Head Teacher Zombie. "Tonight we have reached our goal of reading one million minutes."

"That's one zillion in zombie talk," said Stink.

"I have here a letter signed by none other than the First Lady of the United States. She would like to congratulate all of you for one million minutes of reading. Her letter says, 'Reading grows strong hearts and minds, and you are an inspiration to children everywhere.'"

More clapping!

"People from all over our town who have been coming to the bookshop have pledged to donate books to our school library if we reached our goal. Thanks to every reader, the Virginia Dare School library will be receiving one thousand brand-new books! Hip, hip, hooray!"

"Will they all be zombie books?"

"That's like the whole entire bookshop."

"I'm still reading!" said a zombie firefighter in the corner.

"One last thing." The head teacher tapped on the microphone. She cleared her throat. "I hereby officially declare" – she raised a finger in the air – "that reading is *UN*dead!"

ZOMBIE WALKS

AKA ZOMBIE STOMP, LURCH, STUMBLE, MARCH OR CRAWL

THE FIRST-EVER ZOMBIE WALK WAS HELD IN
SACRAMENTO, CALIFORNIA, IN 2001.

SHALL WE DANCE?
CHECK OUT THE PHILLY ZOMBIE PROM,
HELD EVERY SEPTEMBER IN PHILADELPHIA.

THE FIRST-EVER ZOMBIE WORLD RECORD
WAS SET ON 29 OCTOBER 2006
IN PITTSBURGH, PENNSYLVANIA.
THE WALK OF THE DEAD ATTRACTED
894 ZOMBIES!

4,026 ZOMBIES ATTENDED
THE BIG CHILL FESTIVAL
IN LEDBURY, ENGLAND
ON 6 AUGUST 2009.

DURING THE BRISBANE ZOMBIE WALK,
HELD ON 24 OCTOBER 2010, MORE
THAN 10,000 ZOMBIES MARCHED TO
RAISE MONEY FOR THE BRAIN
FOUNDATION OF AUSTRALIA.

Who's ready for the Midnight Zombie Walk?" asked the bookshop lady.

"We are!"

"Who's going to take over Main Street without fear?"

"Zombies!"

"I can't *hear* you."

"Zombies!"

"Louder!"

"ZOMBIES!" everybody screamed at the top of their lungs.

Zombies lined up at the door. "Cruella De Zombie will lead the way!" said Mrs Tuxedo. "Follow me, if you dare!"

Hordes of zombies poured out on to the pavement. The street was blocked off from traffic. Even Officer Kopp was dressed as a zombie policeman.

Stink and his friends moaned and groaned. Charlie said, "Brains! Me want brains!" They limped and lurched. Stink dragged one foot. Sophie rolled her eyes and stuck out her tongue. Webster drooled.

"Are zombies too cool to drool?" Webster asked.

"You're never too zool to drool," said Sophie.

Riley Rottenburger, Zombie Prom Queen, walked beside them. She wore a bat necklace, long gloves and a crown that looked like a spiderweb. Her sash said LITTLE MISS ZOMBIE.

"Cool crown," said Sophie.

"Thanks. It's a spider tiara," said Riley.

A teenager on a skateboard whizzed past.

"Stare straight ahead," said Stink. "Do not make eye contact with alive humans."

"Keep it weird, dudes," said the skateboarder. Stink cracked up.

Mum and Dad walked behind Stink and his friends.

"Hey! It's the Zombie Lunch Lady!" somebody called. Mum waved.

Zombies filled the streets.

"There must be over a hundred zombies out here," said Mum.

"More like ten hundred," said Stink. "Zen thousand!"

"Did you know zombie walks are a

big thing?" Dad said. "Not just when books come out, either. They have walks like this all over the country. From Pittsburgh to Seattle."

"They even have a world record for the most zombies," said Stink. "Our town should try to break the record for the biggest Midnight Zombie Walk ever."

"I'm going to find Rocky and Frank," said Judy.

"How long is this zombie walk?" Dad asked. "I think rigor mortis is setting in."

"And I know some zombies who are

up way past bedtime," said Mum.

"We can't go home," said Stink. "We haven't even got to the spooky part yet." He pointed down the street. "See? They've turned out all the streetlights on the next three blocks and made it like a haunted house."

"OK, ten more minutes. But as soon as we get home, it's straight to bed," said Mum. "Zombie Lunch Lady has spoken."

"You kids go ahead," said Dad. "Stay with the group, Stink. Mum and I will wait in front of the bookshop."

"Mum? Can you hold Charlie?"

"Sure," said Mum. "We wouldn't want him taking his own midnight walk. He could end up in the coat closet. Or even break one of my fancy dishes." She held Charlie up in front of her face. "And if that happens, you can kiss your allowance goodbye for a while, Charlie," she said to Stink in a funny voice.

Stink's eyes got wide. "We'll talk later," said Mum. "Go and have fun."

A pack of blue-haired zombies in school uniforms lurched down Main Street, past the dark windows of closed shops. Spooky shadows crisscrossed the road like giant cob-webs. Zombie ghosts hung from trees. An owl hooted. The hairs on Stink's arms stood on end.

They walked a little further. Zombie moans and groans filled the air. Body parts littered the pavements. Bloody arms, legs and feet were strewn every which way. All of a sudden, a hand came out of a storm drain. "Aagh!" they screamed, and leapt out of the way.

Hordes of zombies shuffled past Speedy Market, past Fur & Fangs, past Gino's Pizza. Grunts of "Brains" echoed into the night as they lurched

past Screamin' Mimi's, where a voice from inside the shop screamed. And it wasn't for ice cream.

"This is giving me the creeps," Stink whispered. They turned the corner, following behind a bunch of college kids led by an Abe Lincoln zombie.

All of a sudden, a guy dressed as a zombie postman with a beard of blood popped out from behind a postbox. Grinning with decaying teeth, he held up a head. A dead head!

Sophie hung on to Stink's arm. Stink clutched Webster's sleeve. They crept and crawled past the sweet shop. Past the toy store. They were almost back to the bookshop when a bucket of blood and guts rained down in front of them from the roof of the hardware store, gushing all over the pavement.

"Run!" Stink yelled.

The three friends ran screaming down the pavement and around the corner. Webster's shoe tumbled off his head. Sophie dropped Zombalina. Stink lost his brains.

They ran screaming all the way back to the bookshop. To the light. To the spot where Mum, Dad and Judy were waiting for them.

"What's wrong?" asked Dad.

"Are you OK?" said Mum.

"Why were you guys screaming so loud?" Judy asked.

Stink held his side. He bent over. "Body. Parts. Blood," he panted.

"We were screaming because..." Sophie started.

"Because that was the BEST Midnight Zombie Walk EVER!" said Stink.

"Blood and guts and body parts!" said Webster. "We got caught in a *brainstorm*."

"Vomitocious!" said Sophie.

Stink held his hand over his still-beating heart. "I think we just broke the world record! For the first-ever Midnight Zombie RUN!"

ZEE END

10 Things You May Not Know About Megan McDonald

10. The first story Megan ever got published (in the fifth grade) was about a pencil sharpener.

9. She read the biography of Virginia Dare so many times at her school library that the librarian had to ask her to give somebody else a chance.

8. She had to be a boring-old pilgrim every year for Halloween because she has four older sisters, who kept passing their pilgrim costumes down to her.

7. Her favourite board game is the Game of Life.

6. She is a member of the Ice-Cream-for-Life Club at Screamin' Mimi's in her hometown of Sebastopol, California.

5. She has a Band-Aid collection to rival Judy Moody's, including bacon-scented Band-Aids.

4. She owns a jawbreaker that is bigger than a baseball, which she will never, ever eat.

3. Like Stink, she had a pet newt that slipped down the drain when she was his age.

2. She often starts a book by scribbling on a napkin.

1. And the number-one thing you may not know about Megan McDonald is: she was once the opening act for the World's Biggest Cupcake!

10 Things You May Not Know About Peter H. Reynolds

10. He has a twin brother, Paul. Paul was born first, fourteen minutes before Peter decided to arrive.

9. Peter is part owner of a children's book and toy shop called the Blue Bunny in the Massachusetts town where he lives.

8. He's vertically challenged (aka short!).

7. His mother is from England; his father is from Argentina.

6. He made his first animated film while he was in high school.

5. He sometimes paints with tea instead of water – whatever's handy!

4. He keeps a sketch pad and pen on his nightstand. That way, if an idea hits him in the middle of the night, he can jot it down immediately.

3. His favourite candy is a tie between peanut-butter cups and chocolate-covered raisins (same as Megan McDonald!).

2. One of his favourite books growing up was *The Tall Book of Make-Believe* by Jane Werner, illustrated by Garth Williams.

1. And the number-one thing you may not know about Peter H. Reynolds is: he shares a birthday with James Madison, Stink's favourite president!

In the mood for Stink's older sister Judy Moody?

Then try these!

Judy and Stink are starring together!

In full colour!

Think you know Stink?

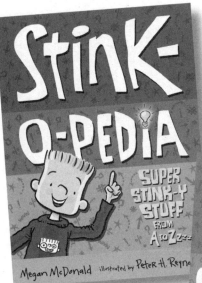

Stink-o-pedia:
*Super Stink-y Stuff
From A to Zzzzz*

Stink-o-pedia 2:
*More Stink-y Stuff
From A to Z*

Stink Moody has his own website!

(One he doesn't have to share with his bossy older sister, Judy)

for the latest in all things Stink, visit

www.stinkmoody.com

where you can:

- Test your Stink knowledge with an I.Q. quiz

- Write and illustrate your own comic strip

- Create your own guinea pig: choose its colours, name it and e-mail it to a friend!

- Guess Stink's middle name

- Learn way-not-boring stuff about Megan McDonald and Peter H. Reynolds

- Read the Stink-y fact of the week!

DOUBLE RARE!

Check out Judy Moody's interactive website at:

www.judymoody.com

Just some of its cool features:

- The Ultimate Judy Moody Fan Quiz

- All-new interactive games and a Mood Meter

- All you need to know about the best-ever Judy Moody Fan Club

- Totally awesome T.P. Club info!

- Digital downloads